Ariel
The Birthday Surprise

By Gail Herman
Illustrated by Studio IBOIX
and Andrea Cagol

DISNEP PRESS
New York

Chapter One

A riel looked around and sighed happily. Sunshine was streaming in through the palace windows. On the dining room table, glasses sparkled and silverware gleamed.

Early morning was Ariel's favorite time of day. Her husband, Prince Eric, sat across the table eating breakfast. He glanced up and smiled. Max the dog lay on the floor nearby.

Ariel piled pancakes and fruit high on her plate. *Being human definitely has its advantages,* she thought. She could even have had waffles and ice cream if she'd wanted to.

"Everything is so peaceful," Ariel said to Eric. "It's so quiet and—"

Crash! Ariel and Eric looked up, startled. Something had banged into a nearby window.

A seagull peeled himself away from the glass and rubbed his beak.

"Scuttle!" Ariel cried. "Are you okay?" She opened the window.

"Clear glass!" Scuttle grumbled as he flew into the room. He smoothed his feathers.

"Hello there, Ariel and Prince Eric." Scuttle bowed clumsily.

Eric laughed. "No need for that, Scuttle. We're all friends."

"Sure, sure," said Scuttle. He glanced at the table. "Is that why you have a nest? You're keeping it for me!"

Eric looked at Ariel, puzzled. But she was used to Scuttle calling human things by the wrong name. When she'd been a mermaid, he'd told her that a fork was called a dinglehopper and humans used it to comb their hair.

Now that she was a human, Ariel had learned what everything was really called.

Ariel smiled and picked up the bread basket. "Take it!" she said. "It's yours!"

"Thanks." Scuttle took the basket, and admired it. "Oh! I just remembered! I was carrying something. I must have lost it when I hit the glass. Now, where can it be?"

Scuttle flew outside, then back inside. He searched up and down and all around. Finally, he landed on the window ledge.

A card was tucked under his wing.

"For you," he told Ariel.

The princess opened the card. "Why, it's an invitation!" she exclaimed. "Adella is having a birthday party today."

Ariel had six mermaid sisters, and Adella was one of them. Mermaid birthdays were always fun. Eagerly, Ariel read the card:

Come Under the Sea!

Why: To help Adella celebrate her birthday!
When: Today! All day, all night. It's a sleepover!
Where: The royal palace in Atlantica
What else: A special birthday concert

"Of course I'll come," Ariel said.

"I'll deliver the news," the seagull said, flying off.

Ariel stood up. "I'd better get ready," she told Eric. "I have to bring a present. Maybe that music box I saw in the village . . ." Her voice trailed off. "Oh, Eric, I'll miss you. Maybe I should stay here. . . ."

Prince Eric reached for her hand. "Of course you should be with your family, Ariel. Max and I will be fine on our own."

Woof, woof, Max whimpered.

"Come on, Max," Eric said. "I'll miss her, too. But it won't be so bad. After all, it's just for one night!"

Chapter Two

*B*efore she left, Ariel took a quick trip to the village. She found the music box in a small corner shop.

On the lid, a beautiful mermaid spun around. When Ariel opened the box, it played a pretty song.

Adella would love it.

Soon it was time to say good-bye. Ariel

kissed Eric and hugged Max. Then she waded into the ocean.

"Father!" she called. "Are you here?"

King Triton came to the surface of the water.

"Hello, Ariel!" Triton said, beaming. "Are you ready for Adella's party?" Ariel nodded, and her father waved his magic trident.

Suddenly Ariel's human clothes and legs were gone, and she was a mermaid again. She dove into a wave, happy to be in the sea.

A second later, she surfaced. "Good-bye, Eric! See you tomorrow!" Her husband blew her a kiss, and Max barked.

Ariel dove again and followed her father toward the royal palace.

"Ariel, I must do some work now," Triton

said. "There have been reports of a shark swimming near Atlantica."

Triton hugged Ariel, then hurried off. A shark! That could mean trouble, Ariel knew. But it was so beautiful here. Sunshine slanted through the water. Colorful flowers swayed in the current. It was hard to think about danger.

"Ariel, Ariel! You're back!" The mermaid's good friend Flounder the fish raced over. "I wasn't sure . . . I mean I hoped . . . and you are. Here, I mean."

Flounder was so excited. He could barely finish a sentence. Darting here and there, he peeked over his shoulder at Ariel. *Bam!* He swam smack into a patch of prickly plants.

"Ouch!"

"Don't move," Ariel told him. "I'll get you out." She carefully pulled the leaves apart, and Flounder paddled backward until he was free. Then they headed toward the palace.

"I'm glad to see you, too, Flounder!" Ariel told her friend.

She and Flounder still saw each other a lot. He liked to splash around the lagoon at her castle. But it was different under the sea. They could swim anywhere and go exploring, just like they used to.

Up ahead, Ariel could see the palace. She spotted the mother-of-pearl staircase, the long, flowing plants, and the glittering gems. She sighed happily.

"I found an amazing treasure the other day," Flounder chattered on. "It's in a new shipwreck. I was swimming along as usual, and suddenly—"

"Ariel! Ariel!" All of her sisters swam to meet her.

"Happy birthday, Adella!" Ariel exclaimed as she hugged her sister.

"You're really here!" Adella whispered. "I've got so many plans for today. Girl talk. An afternoon at the spa. And, of course, the birthday concert!"

Adella held up a long scroll. The paper unrolled and hit the ocean floor.

"It's a list of everything I want to do, get, and see on my birthday," Adella told Ariel. "I've checked off some things already!"

Adella began to read out loud:

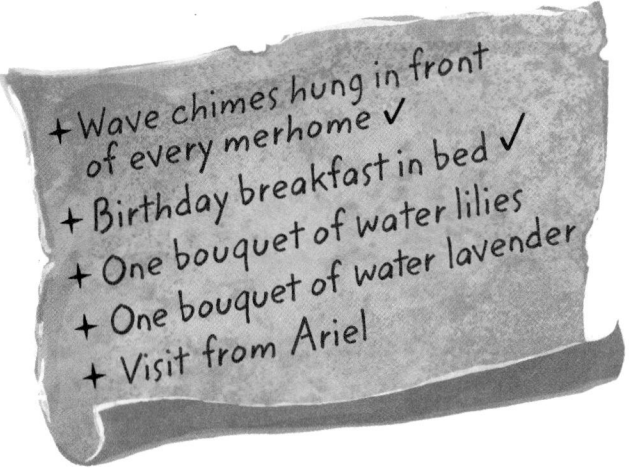

+ Wave chimes hung in front of every merhome ✓
+ Birthday breakfast in bed ✓
+ One bouquet of water lilies
+ One bouquet of water lavender
+ Visit from Ariel

Adella stopped. "I'll just check that off now," she said. Then she continued:

+ Lunch with all my sisters
+ Birthday cake
+ Seaweed body wrap at the merspa
+ Concert rehearsal
+ Concert

"Stop talking for just one minute, Adella," Andrina interrupted. "Let us say hello!" She kissed Ariel's cheek.

Arista kissed her other cheek. Attina squeezed Ariel's hand.

Aquata and Alana swam around Ariel, making swirls of bubbles. Before long it was so bubbly that they bumped into each other!

They rubbed their heads.

"Watch where you're going!"

"I was watching!"

"You weren't watching!"

"Was, too!"

"Girls!" said King Triton, who had just returned to the palace. "Come inside. Let Ariel get settled. Then you can start the festivities.

"Sebastian!" he boomed. "You're running the show today. When do the festivities start?"

A crab hurried over and nodded at Ariel.

"Welcome back," Sebastian said in a lilting voice. "The festivities begi-i-i-n . . ." He drew out the word to build excitement. "Now!"

Chapter Three

$\mathcal{T}$wo young merchildren swam into the castle's great hall. They carried a huge bouquet of water lilies. The flowers were so big, Ariel could barely see the children who were holding them.

"Lovely!" exclaimed Adella. "Just what I wanted."

Sebastian tapped his claw impatiently. He

had everything planned to the minute. The crab was determined to keep the day on schedule. That way, the concert would be just in time for sunset.

The morning was filled with mermaid talk and opening presents. Then, at precisely 1:01, the sisters finished lunch.

"So far, so good," Sebastian told Ariel.

"It's time for the Sea Swirl Spa!" Adella said. "I can't wait. My tail always sparkles after a beauty treatment."

"The deep-sea mud is terrific for my face!" Andrina added.

"The best," agreed Arista.

"It's wonderfully refreshing," said Attina.

"But there are only six deep-sea clam beds," Adella put in.

"And seven of us!" Alana cried, horrified.

"You shouldn't get the treatment," Aquata told Alana.

"No! You're the one who shouldn't get it," Alana told Aquata.

"No, you."

"No, *you!* "

"It's okay!" Ariel raised her voice to be heard. "I won't go."

"But Ariel, you're our guest!" said Adella.

"Really, Adella. It's fine. I want to spend a little time with Flounder anyway," Ariel assured her.

"Okay, everyone!" Sebastian clapped his claws. "Let's get moving! We have a schedule to keep." He turned to Ariel. "I'll be going with your sisters. To keep everyone in line . . . I mean, on time."

"Don't worry, Sebastian." Ariel swam away from her sisters. "I'm leaving right now. And I'll be back in plenty of time for the rehearsal."

Sebastian raised an eyebrow. When Ariel swam off to do her own thing, she always lost track of time.

Ariel did think she had plenty of time. Flounder and I will do a little exploring, she told herself. Then I'll go straight to the concert hall.

"Come on, Flounder!" she said. Together, they raced toward a shipwreck.

Flounder swam through a broken porthole. "Come, look at this, Ariel!"

Flounder pointed at a blue vase.

"Adella would love this," Ariel said. "She can put the water lilies in it." Just then, her eyes fell on something. She picked it up and glanced nervously at Flounder.

"It's a shark's tooth," the fish said.

A shiver ran down Ariel's spine. Those shark sightings her father had told her about—they were for real!

Still, it was a beautiful day, and Ariel didn't want to waste it worrying. She and Flounder met up with their old friends, the sea horses and the dolphins. They swam around Atlantica all morning.

Ariel was chasing a sponge ball, playing keep-away with a dolphin, when—*blam!*—she turned suddenly and swam right into Sebastian.

"Sebastian! Where did you come from?" she asked.

"From the concert hall!" Sebastian said, frowning and out of breath. "Everyone's waiting!"

Chapter Four

The rehearsal! Ariel remembered. How had time gone by so fast?

With a flip of her tail and a wave to her old friends, Ariel was on her way.

Moments later, she reached the concert hall. Adella, Andrina, Arista, Attina, Aquata, and Alana were already there, but they weren't singing.

"I should do that solo," Aquata was saying.

"No, I should," Alana told her.

"No, me."

"No, me."

"I'm sorry I'm late!" Ariel interrupted. "But we still have plenty of time to rehearse."

Adella gasped.

"Really," Ariel insisted, puzzled by her sister's reaction, "we have plenty of time."

"It's not that," Adella whispered. "There's a shark."

Ariel turned her head slowly. She held her breath.

A shark hovered at the edge of the hall. His long tail whipped back and forth. His beady eyes stared straight ahead.

Ariel's heart thumped loudly. She was

sure the shark could hear it.

"What do you think we should do?" whispered Andrina.

Ariel knew they shouldn't shout for help. That might make the shark attack.

Should they stay still? Maybe he'd get bored and swim away.

Ariel signaled her sisters. The mermaids froze in place. Seconds passed, then minutes. Time crawled by. After a while, Ariel's muscles began to ache.

And then she felt a sneeze coming on.

A sneeze! Ariel groaned. Why did she have to sneeze right now?

Ariel pinched her nose and tried to hold back the sneeze. Just then, the shark opened its great mouth. Razor-sharp teeth glinted.

He reared up, then sped through the water . . . right past the mermaids, into the open ocean.

"Whew!" Ariel cried. Then she sneezed. "Aa-aa-aaachoo!"

"That was way too close!" said Adella. She took a deep breath.

"I wonder how he got by the guards," Andrina said.

"Anyway, it's over," said Aquata. "And it's time for me to sing that solo!"

Alana glared at her, and Ariel wondered how they would ever make it through the rehearsal.

That evening, Sebastian paced back and forth in front of his music stand. He wanted everything to go well. "All right, everyone!" He tapped his baton. "The audience will be arriving any minute."

The mermaids got in place. Soon,

undersea creatures great and small filled the hall. It was showtime!

Ariel and her sisters performed song after song. The dolphins flapped their flippers, and King Triton tapped his trident against the floor.

"Now for the big finish!" Sebastian announced.

Onstage, Adella hovered above the others. She smiled down as they sang "Happy Birthday."

Andrina sang a line, then Arista and Attina chimed in.

Aquata and Alana sang together since they hadn't been able to decide who got a solo.

Then Sebastian pointed up. All the

merpeople and sea creatures swam to the surface. The sun was setting. Blazing red and orange colors painted the sky.

Adella's sisters sang the last line with a quick solo by Ariel.

Applause rang out. "Hear, hear!" cried the merpeople.

Ariel turned to her sister, smiling. "Happy birthday, Adella."

"Oh, Ariel!" Adella said. "It's so good to have you home. I wish you'd never leave."

Adella's words echoed around the shore. They bounced from rock to rock and hung in the air. A curtain of darkness fell. One moment, the sky was light. The next instant, it was black as midnight.

Fish scattered.

Ariel's sisters held on to each other fearfully. Then, holding hands, they ducked below the surface, too.

Still at the surface, King Triton rose to his full height. Ariel was by his side.

"Father!" Ariel gasped. "The sun!"

The sun had turned into a black disk. A fiery ring of light circled it, like a sparkling crown.

Triton held his trident tightly. "Now I understand," he murmured. "It's so rare."

"What is? What is it?"

"A solar eclipse." Triton's voice was strained. "The moon blocks the entire sun! It's a dangerous, mysterious time. I don't know what will happen," he warned. "We need to be very, very careful."

Suddenly, the water turned rough. Waves rose high, then higher still. The current grew strong. Ariel felt herself pushed and pulled.

"Father!" she cried. A giant wave rolled toward her, gathering merpeople, fish, driftwood, and plants with it. Then it tossed everyone and everything around.

Ariel tried to stay afloat. She looked frantically for her father and sisters. But the wave's powerful force kept pulling her down.

Crash! Ariel landed on something hard. Ariel couldn't see a thing. She couldn't tell where she was. She tried to get up. But a hard object knocked her over, pinning her to the ground.

Ariel couldn't move.

Chapter Five

*T*ime passed. Slowly, the dark waters grew lighter. The sea grew calm. At last, Ariel could see.

I'm on the deck of a ship, she thought.

The ship's helm, round and solid, held her in place. She squirmed. But she knew it was impossible to escape.

"Hello?" she called out.

She waited a moment. "Hello?" she called again.

"Ariel!" Flounder hurried over. "We've been looking for you everywhere! Are you all right?"

Ariel pulled at the wheel. It wouldn't budge. "I'm fine. I just need to move this."

Flounder swam under the wheel. He pushed at the same time Ariel pulled.

The wheel lifted slightly, and Ariel slipped free. "Whew!" She gazed around. The ocean floor was littered with broken planks, uprooted sea grass, and shattered shells.

"Should we clean up around here?" Flounder pushed some broken planks to the side. He swept up the wooden bits with his fin. But Ariel was already speeding away.

"I need to find Father so he can change me back. I've got to return to the surface. Eric will be worried!"

At the palace, King Triton sat on his throne. The sea chair was still in one piece. But there were cracks in the pillars. Stones and sea glass lay scattered across the floor.

Sebastian stepped gingerly over the broken bits.

"All octopuses! You're assigned to the far east corner. You'll be on cleanup duty, picking up wreckage. Please use all arms. Squid! You'll be mopping up in the kitchen. Ariel! Join your sisters in the—"

"Oh! Ariel!" Sebastian interrupted himself. "Flounder found you!"

Ariel nodded, taking in the damage.

37

"Thank goodness you're safe," said Triton, pulling his daughter in close. "Thank goodness everyone is."

Ariel breathed a sigh of relief.

"I'm glad. But I need to go home," Ariel told her father. "I want to make sure Eric and everyone at the castle are fine. Can you please change me back into a human?"

Triton nodded. "Follow me."

Together they swam to the surface. Moonbeams bright as sun rays lit the ocean. Triton led Ariel to a rock near the shore. He raised his trident.

One lone spark flew from its tip.

Ariel looked down. Her tail swished in the water.

"Where are my legs?"

King Triton shook his head. An uncertain look clouded his eyes. "I'll try again."

Once more, he raised his trident toward the sky. But it fizzled again.

"Ah, Ariel," Triton said sadly. "I'm afraid I can't do it."

"But, why?"

"The solar eclipse," Triton explained. "Adella made her birthday wish just as the eclipse took place. She wished you could stay. And the eclipse was so strong . . . so magical . . . that her wish came true. My powers aren't enough to change you back."

Ariel stared at her father. "But that means I'll never be able to leave. I'll never be human. I'll always be a mermaid!"

Triton gazed at her and nodded slowly.

Ariel choked back a sob. "No," she whispered.

"Ariel!" Eric was calling from the shore. "You're safe! I saw the eclipse and the giant waves! I've been walking along the shore looking for you."

In a flash, Ariel dove from the rock into the water, toward Eric.

He splashed into the water to meet her.

"Oh, Eric," she cried, "I'm so glad to see you! Is everyone at the castle all right?"

He nodded. "There's some damage to the east wing that I should attend to. Are you ready?"

"I can't turn back into a human!" Tearfully, she explained what happened.

"That can't be true!" Eric cried.

King Triton neared them. "I'm afraid it is," he told Eric. He looked at Ariel sadly. "I'm sorry. I feel so helpless. You know I'd do anything to make you happy."

"I know, Father."

Triton was quiet for a moment. Then he said, "There is one thing we could try."

"Yes?" said Ariel eagerly.

"You must spend tomorrow as if it were today. As if it were Adella's birthday all over again—from when you first saw your sisters to the moment Adella made the wish. If the feeling is there . . . if the feeling is strong enough . . . then the solar eclipse will occur again, and Adella can change her wish."

Repeat the day? Ariel thought. The whole day, and everything that happened? "That would be impossible!" she exclaimed.

King Triton shook his head. "Nothing is impossible."

"What do you mean, if the feeling's there?"

"All I can tell you is that you have the best shot of turning back into a human if you and your sisters pretend it is today when you wake up tomorrow morning," Triton answered.

Ariel's mind raced. She'd alert the kingdom. Ask every merperson, every sea creature, to copy everything they had done. She'd make sure her sisters did all of the same things. She'd make sure Adella believed, really and truly, that it was her birthday all over again.

"Tonight, you must sleep in the guest grotto," Triton told Ariel. "Right after breakfast, come to the meeting hall, as you did this morning. And then we'll begin."

Ariel and Eric looked at each other and nodded. It was their only hope of being together again.

Chapter Six

Quickly, Ariel found her sisters and explained the situation. "Tomorrow we must celebrate Adella's birthday all over again. It has to be exactly the same!"

Next, she sent word throughout the kingdom: "Tomorrow will be Princess Adella's birthday for the second time in a row! Hang the wave chimes and banners!"

Then, Ariel turned back the hands of the kingdom clock. The old grandfather clock had tumbled from a ship long ago, but it still kept perfect time. For good measure, Ariel flipped over a giant hourglass that would measure a whole day.

"There," she said. "Everything is set one day back. When I wake up in the morning, it will be Adella's birthday again."

Ariel swam to the grotto. The cave was cozy, with a snug moss bed, and a lanternfish was casting a soft glow. Still, Ariel felt lonely. And the grotto was so different from her bedroom. In fact . . . it felt a little spooky.

Strange shadows danced against the wall. Then she heard an eerie squeaking noise. Maybe she should find somewhere else to sleep . . . maybe even in her old bed in the castle. She could sneak away before Adella woke up.

Splash! Ariel sat up.

What was that noise? She heard something swimming toward her. No . . . more than one something. She could make out shapes now. Whatever they were, they were coming closer and closer.

"Ariel," one of them said.

It was Sebastian and Flounder! Ariel slumped back on the moss.

"We came to keep you company," Flounder told her.

"We thought you might be scared," Sebastian added.

"You were absolutely right!" Ariel said.

Even with her friends nearby, Ariel didn't sleep that well. She was worried. Would everything go as planned? Would Adella really think it was her birthday?

Should she lure the shark back? Or would she be putting everyone in danger?

At last, the first rays of sun lit the water.

Ariel waited until the sun rose higher. Soon it was midmorning. That's the time I swam down, she thought.

"Sebastian and Flounder!" she called. "Let's go!"

The three friends swam past merhomes. Sparkling wave chimes were blowing in the current, the same as yesterday. Fresh banners hung across rocks and ledges, with HAPPY BIRTHDAY, ADELLA! written in bold letters.

Sea horses trumpeted, "It's Adella's birthday! Happy birthday, Princess Adella!"

"Princess Ariel! Hello!" people called. Everyone sounded surprised and pleased to see her. It felt like yesterday all over again.

They were all trying so hard!

When Ariel arrived at the palace, her

sisters gathered around, just as they had before. "We're really excited!" Adella whispered. "We get to do this twice."

Everyone giggled. Ariel was glad they wanted to help. But this wasn't a game.

Ariel turned to Adella. A lovely coral necklace hung from her neck. "You're wearing the present from Father," she whispered. "He didn't give it to you until lunchtime." Ariel thought a moment. "Yesterday you wore a shell necklace!"

"Can't I just keep it on?" Adella pleaded. "It's such a small thing, really."

Ariel sighed. She hated to disappoint Adella. But she wanted everything to be as perfect as possible.

Adella looked at Ariel's face. "I'm sorry,

Ariel! Of course I'll change it!" She whirled away. When she came back, she was wearing her simple shell necklace.

"Now, your list!" Ariel whispered.

Adella looked around. "Uh-oh," she said. "Where is it?" She nudged Andrina, who nudged Arista, who nudged Attina.

Attina nudged Aquata, and Aquata nudged Alana.

"Must I do everything?" Sebastian hurried over with the scroll. Then he saw Ariel looking at him sadly. He wanted her to be happy. "Of course, Ariel, I will do this for you. I will try my hardest to keep everything in order."

A few minutes later, some merchildren arrived with a bouquet of sea lavender.

"Oh, it's lovely!" said Adella. She buried her nose in the flowers.

Ariel got a funny feeling. Something seemed off. The flowers were supposed to be water lilies! The sea lavender came in the afternoon!

"Take it away!" she whispered to the children.

The merchildren scurried off.

Adella smiled sheepishly.

Seconds later, the children returned with water lilies. "Oh, how nice!" Adella said.

Ariel smiled at her sister.

Next, Sebastian read over the schedule. Then Ariel went to the sisters' bedroom. She had relaxed here for a bit before the festivities began. But now she could only pace back and forth. Let's see . . . what had she done yesterday?

She straightened her moss blanket. She combed her hair. She went through some old books she kept in a drawer. This time, she came across a favorite fairy tale.

"Oh!" she said. *"The Princess and the Puffer Fish!"*

She began to read.

A while later, she closed the cover and stretched.

All at once, she jumped up! She'd been so caught up in the story that she'd completely lost track of time.

She rushed to the dining hall.

"Five minutes late, as usual," her father said with a frown.

Then Sebastian frowned. He tried so hard to keep everyone on schedule.

Ariel grinned.

It was perfectly fine. She'd been a little late for lunch on Adella's birthday, too!

Chapter Seven

At lunch, Ariel made sure Adella sat next to King Triton. Then she ushered her other sisters into the seats they'd had yesterday.

"I've been practicing the solo for 'Sea to Shining Sea,'" Alana announced.

"That's my solo!" Aquata protested.

"There's still time to change," said Alana.

"No, there's not."

"Yes, there is."

"No."

"Yes."

Will those two never stop bickering? Ariel wondered. She rose to sit between them. But then she sat back down. Alana and Aquata had been seated next to each other yesterday. So they had to sit like that today, too.

The merchildren brought the bouquet of lavender. Then the chef carried in seaweed noodles, piled high on plates, just like the day before. Then came the kelp cake, decorated with tiny shells.

"My favorite!" Adella cried.

King Triton gave Adella his present again. She squealed happily. "A coral necklace. Just what I wanted!" She put on the necklace at once.

Ariel grinned. Adella was as excited today as she'd been yesterday! It was almost as if she'd forgotten she was pretending.

"Now!" Adella smiled at Ariel. "Don't you have something for me?"

"Of course!" Ariel held out a box. Sebastian had taken the music box from Adella's nightstand earlier.

Eagerly, Adella opened the gift. "It's a music box!" she squealed. She gazed at the tiny mermaid on top. "I have the same one!"

"It *is* the same one!" hissed Sebastian.

"Oh, right. Sorry," Adella said.

Soon lunch ended. "Well, time for our beauty treatment!" said Adella.

More than anything, Ariel wanted to keep an eye on things and make sure her sisters did everything they'd done yesterday. But right now she needed to go exploring with Flounder.

The sisters left, giggling. Ariel glanced at the clock. It was 1:01. Perfect.

"Do you know where Sebastian is?" Ariel asked Flounder.

"Coming, coming," Sebastian said, scuttling over. "Don't worry, I'm going to the spa. I was just checking my timetable. We're right on schedule."

"Good. But can you sneak away from Adella and report back to me about the spa? I'll be near the new shipwreck with Flounder."

Ariel and Flounder swam toward the shipwreck. But Ariel kept looking back. She couldn't stop wondering, What is Adella doing now? Is everything the same?

The friends paddled around the shipwreck, looking in all of the nooks for treasure. Then they swam to meet the sea horses and dolphins.

"Anyone for a game of keep away?" called Flounder.

Ariel was chasing the sponge ball when she heard a loud *"Pssst!"*

She turned around. She saw a strange crab with long curly hair. She looked at him, puzzled.

"Ariel, it's me!" The crab lifted its hair.

"Sebastian?" the little mermaid said, shocked.

"Yes, of course it's Sebastian. I am wearing a wig. Thanks to the Sea Swirl Spa, I'm in the middle of a makeover."

Ariel giggled. "You look lovely. Did you do this yesterday, too?"

Sebastian turned an even deeper shade of red. "I an sorry to say that they made me. At least then I didn't have to parade all over the ocean!"

Ariel turned serious. "Thank you for helping, Sebastian. What is Adella doing right now?"

"She's trying on wigs, too. They all are."

Ariel nodded. "Good. That's exactly the

same." She shooed the crab away. "Now go back to the spa!"

Sebastian swam away. The game continued. Ariel and Flounder tossed the sponge around.

A little later, Sebastian returned. He still wore the wig. But this time, he had on long fake eyelashes and the tips of his claws were purple.

"They're getting their eyes done!" he whispered.

Ariel giggled and pointed at his claws.

"It's manicure time," he explained before swimming off.

After a while, Sebastian returned. "Your sisters are having facials," he reported. His own shell was now almost completely covered with deep-sea mud. "Everything has been exactly the same. This is the last part of the beauty treatment."

Sebastian swam away with a wave. "Now for my massage!" he called back. "Please do not disturb."

When Sebastian didn't return, Ariel knew she had to do something to get the sisters back on track, even if it was a little different than yesterday. "I'm going to the spa," she told Flounder. She took a deep breath, hoping this wouldn't affect the spell.

Ariel dashed through the water. Minutes later, she neared the Sea Swirl Spa. Her sisters lay back in clamshell beds, their faces covered with hot towels.

The mermaids were so quiet. In the silence, Ariel heard a soft noise.

"Zzzzz."

"Zzzzz."

Her sisters had fallen asleep! Ariel pulled Sebastian off his massage table.

"Ariel! What are you doing? I was finally relaxing!"

"We have to wake up my sisters!" she whispered. "We're going to be late for the rehearsal." She pulled at a vine and gave another one to Sebastian. "Hold on to this. Come on!"

Ariel and Sebastian floated above the sisters. Their vines trailed in the water.

"One, two, three," whispered Ariel. They dangled the vines around the sisters, brushing the mermaids gently.

"Hey, stop tickling me!" Aquata said to Alana.

"No, you stop tickling me," Alana told Aquata.

"You stop!"

"No, you!"

"Oh, no!" Adella sat up with a start. "We need to hurry! We have to rehearse!"

Ariel grinned. But right away, her smile

faded. The rehearsal! That was when the shark almost attacked.

She knew her father had ordered shark patrols. Fish, dolphins, and more were swimming along the borders of Atlantica. The shark couldn't just wander by the concert hall the way it had before.

Of course, Ariel could lure the shark to the hall. But should she put her sisters in danger?

All day long, Ariel knew she'd have to make this decision.

Then she realized she'd known what she was going to do all along. She wouldn't bait the shark. She couldn't ask her sisters to face that kind of danger—again! After all, what if they got hurt? She'd never forgive herself, even if it meant she couldn't be human.

"We'll do this rehearsal like we did before," Ariel told the mermaids as they swam to the hall. "But this time, without the shark."

"Oh, but Ariel!" said Adella. "That's not how it was at all. You said everything had to be exactly the same."

Ariel nodded. "I did say that. But it's too big a risk. What if the shark attacked us this time?"

She thought of Eric. Of Max. Of their last breakfast . . . and how they might never be together again.

Ariel's voice caught in her throat, and a tear trickled down her cheek. "The danger is too great."

Chapter Eight

riel swam away from the others. She needed to be by herself for a few moments. Resting on a rock, she thought things over.

She pulled a pink flower from her hair— Eric had given it to her just before she had left the surface. She loved Eric and wanted to be with him. But she loved her family, too.

I have to stay strong, she told herself. I'll just do the best I can. And if that isn't enough . . . well . . .

She'd think about that later. There! Ariel put the flower back in her hair. She did feel a bit better.

Slowly, she made her way back to the concert hall.

"Hi, Ariel!" called her sisters from inside.

Ariel waved her tail, then stopped to concentrate. Maybe if they copied everything perfectly from here on in . . . word for word, action for action . . . they wouldn't even need the shark.

"I'm sorry I'm late!" she called out.

Let's see, she thought. What came next? How did we start the first time?

No one did much of anything, she remembered. The sisters floated this way and that. Ariel looked around. Good, everyone was doing just that.

Then Sebastian came in, as if on cue. No one paid the slightest attention to him.

"Ignored yesterday," Sebastian muttered. "Ignored today."

Ariel smiled, then turned around so the crab wouldn't see her.

The concert would begin with "Ode to the Reef." "Sing Out, Sister" would follow, then "Sea to Shining Sea." The grand ending, of course, would be "Happy Birthday."

Ariel swam up to the stage. She floated next to Adella. Adella was next to Andrina, who was next to Arista, who was next to Attina, who—

"Wait!" Ariel cried suddenly as Sebastian raised his baton. "Where are Aquata and Alana?" They had disappeared!

The other sisters exchanged looks.

"Do you know?" Ariel asked.

The mermaids kept silent. Finally,

Andrina said, "Oh, who cares, anyway? I'm so tired of their bickering."

"Yes," Arista agreed. "They're probably in a huff somewhere. They might never ever show up!"

Ariel studied her sisters. Their voices were strained. Adella tapped her tail nervously. Attina twirled a strand of hair around her finger. They were all jittery.

Something was going on.

Just then, Aquata and Alana darted in.

"We're here!" Alana said, out of breath.

Aquata looked over her shoulder. "Let's get started. Quickly!"

What was the rush? Ariel wondered. Then she shook her head. It didn't make a difference, anyway. She had to concentrate on the rehearsal to make it an exact copy of yesterday's.

"It's not that bad," she remembered to say. "We still have plenty of time—"

"Don't move!" Adella hissed. "There's a shark."

Ariel nodded. "Excellent idea!" she whispered. She hadn't thought of *pretending* to see a shark. They'd act as if a shark were really there. Then she noticed that her sisters looked pale.

Slowly, she turned.

A shark hovered among the vines at the edge of the hall. It was the same one as yesterday!

Ariel gasped. "How did it get in?" she asked softly. "What about the shark patrol?"

"Alana talked to the swordfish on duty," whispered Aquata. "So he wasn't paying attention."

"And Aquata led the shark right here," Alana went on softly.

Ariel couldn't believe it. Her sisters had risked their lives for her!

"We knew you'd say not to do it," said Aquata. "So we didn't tell you."

"We all agreed," Andrina said proudly. Then she looked puzzled. "Now what are we going to do?"

"We do what we did yesterday," Ariel said. "Wait it out."

Chapter Nine

Minutes passed, and Ariel stayed as still as she could. At least this time, Ariel didn't have to sneeze. Then, just as before, the shark opened its great jaws.

Would the shark swim past the mermaids again? Or would it attack?

The shark watched the mermaids. Then it lunged.

"Over here, Sharky!" A red claw waved in front of the shark. The shark stopped.

"Come and get your favorite meal. Crab à la Sebastian!"

The shark snapped at Sebastian. But the crab was whisked behind a stone pillar. Flounder had pulled him to safety!

The shark kept going. He searched for the tasty morsel, until he disappeared in a haze of bubbles.

Ariel hugged her sisters tight.

Sebastian and Flounder swam out, smiling. "Well, now that's taken care of, let's begin the rehearsal," Sebastian said in a businesslike way.

"Sisters, Sebastian, Flounder! How can I ever thank—" Ariel began.

But Sebastian waved his claw. "Didn't you hear me? It's time to begin the rehearsal."

The crab raised his baton. "I think you were on the left, Aquata, and Alana was on the right."

"No," said Aquata. "I was on the right."

"Left," said Alana.

"Right."

"Left."

This time, Ariel didn't even try to stop her sisters. They could argue all day if they wanted, after leading the shark there. A few minutes later, the sisters continued with the rehearsal. Ariel tried to stay calm.

In just a little while, she'd find out if the plan had worked—if repeating the day could bring back the eclipse, even though it hadn't been *exactly* the same. Would it be enough for Adella to get the chance to change her birthday wish?

The concert hall was filling up. Merpeople flitted about finding seats. Fish and dolphins swam here and there, looking for the best views. Lobsters and snails made their way along the seafloor.

The Undersea Orchestra moved to the stage. Sea horses held their trumpets. Eels slithered by their drums. Fish flexed their fins to play their harps.

King Triton entered the hall and sat down front and center. Sebastian nodded, then stepped onto the stage.

"Thank you!" Sebastian said.

No one noticed the crab, though. The audience murmured and chattered. *"Thank you!"* Sebastian said, louder.

Everyone kept talking.

Finally, King Triton raised his trident. Silence fell.

"Thank you," Sebastian said. "I am pleased to lead the Undersea Orchestra for a very special event—Princess Adella's birthday!"

The audience cheered.

The curtains parted. Everyone gasped, although they'd just seen the backdrop the day before.

Sea anemones rose from the ocean floor. On each one stood a princess, smiling and singing.

"Joy to the seas," they sang sweetly. *"Let's all sing, please. And everyone is glad!"*

The mermaids floated away from the anemones. They linked arms. Aquata and Alana smiled at one another. Adella glowed with happiness.

The song ended. The audience rose to its tails. "More! Encore!" they cried.

The sisters sang "Sing Out, Sister," then "Sea to Shining Sea." Each song drew greater applause.

Finally, Ariel waved for quiet.

"I'm so happy to be here for Adella's birthday," she announced.

Adella blew a kiss across the water. And Ariel realized that in spite of everything, she was happy to be with her family. She felt

happy to celebrate with them all over again. If only she knew she'd be human tomorrow . . .

Ariel tossed her hair. Don't think about that now, she told herself. Concentrate on the moment. On Adella's birthday.

"Happy birthday, dear sister," Ariel said. She signaled the others to start the last song.

The sisters began to sing.

The mermaids burst through the water to the surface for Ariel's final solo. Just as before, the sun was setting. Orange and red colors lined the sky. Everything looked the same.

Ariel sang the last line.

Adella swam to her side. "Oh, Ariel!" she said. "It's so good to have you home—"

Ariel gasped. Was Adella going to say she

wished she'd never leave? Again? This was the time to say something different. To change the wish!

Ariel glimpsed Eric on the beach. She touched Adella's arm and pointed to her husband.

"But I wish you could be where you are most happy," Adella continued, "your own home."

At that moment, darkness fell. The sun disappeared behind the moon. Only its fiery edges peeked out.

It was the solar eclipse!

Suddenly, the waves grew higher and higher. The wind whistled and blew. Merpeople were tossed here and there. Ariel felt herself lifted up on a giant wave. It carried her away from the others. Away from her family. Away from the sea. This time, it brought her toward the shore. Slowly, the water ebbed, leaving her lying on soft sand.

Ariel opened her eyes. Her tail was gone. She had legs! Real human legs!

"Ariel!" Eric rushed across the beach. "You're here! You're back!"

Ariel stood and wobbled just a bit. Then she straightened herself and held her head high.

"Yes!" she said as the sun came out from behind the moon. The shore blazed with light. And Ariel glowed with joy.

"Yes, I am!" she exclaimed. She waved to her sisters and father, and Sebastian and Flounder. "Thank you, everyone!" she shouted. "This means the world to me." Then she walked with Eric back to their castle.

Chapter Ten

Days passed, then weeks. Often, Ariel dreamed of the solar eclipse. She'd see the moon in front of the sun. She'd see giant waves in a sea as black as midnight. Then she'd wake up, happy to be with Eric. Happy to be human.

Almost every morning, Ariel would walk along the water's edge. She'd wave to the seagulls. She'd call for her sisters. They'd wave and chatter across the water.

One day, she and Eric took a boat ride. First Ariel rowed. Then it was Eric's turn. He was lifting an oar when Scuttle landed on its edge.

"Hello, Ariel! Hello, Prince Eric!"

"Scuttle! How many times do I have to tell you? Please call me Eric!"

"Of course, Prince Eric," the seagull replied.

Ariel laughed. "Do you have something for me?" she asked.

"Oh! That's right. I do!" Scuttle patted his feathers. "Now, where did I put that thing?"

"Here, Scuttle!" Flounder jumped out of the water, a piece of paper in his mouth. "It's

a card!" He bobbed for a moment, while Ariel took the paper.

"Why, thank you, Flounder."

Ariel read the card to herself. Then she read it again, just to make sure she had it right.

"It's a birthday invitation!" she said.

Eric groaned. "Not another one!"

"This time, it's for Andrina." Ariel sighed. Of course she wanted to go. Andrina was her sister! But how could she be a mermaid again? The eclipse was too fresh in her mind.

"You should go, Ariel!" said Scuttle. "There couldn't possibly be another solar eclipse."

Maybe not, Ariel thought. But what if something else happened? What if her father's trident didn't work for another reason?

On the other hand, it would be an adventure. And how could she say no to that?

"You're not going, are you?" asked Eric.

Ariel felt torn. "I don't know. The invitation doesn't give much information. It doesn't say where it is. Or how long."

"Oh!" Scuttle fluttered his wings. "I forgot! There's another part of the invite!"

He patted his feathers again.

"Okay, okay, Sebastian must come to the rescue once again." The crab poked his head out of the water. Then he scrambled onto a rock.

He waved a wrinkled paper in his claw. "For you, Ariel."

Sebastian glared at Scuttle. "It was just floating on a wave. It would've washed out to sea, if I hadn't stumbled across it. Good thing—"

"Thank you, Sebastian," said Ariel. She took the paper, and smoothed it on her knee.

"Ahh!" she cried happily. "I'll definitely go to the party! Without a doubt!"

"You will?" said Prince Eric.

"Yes!"

Ariel's six sisters suddenly popped out of the water. They swam around the boat.

"It's in Crystal Cove!" explained Aquata.

"There's plenty of land," said Andrina.

"And sand," added Arista.

"And water," Attina put in.

"We can all be together!" said Adella and Alana.

"And Ariel can still be human," Andrina added.

"You can come, too," Ariel told Eric with a smile.

"Please, join us! You are welcome!" King Triton boomed as he surfaced.

Ariel reached over to hug her sisters one

by one. The boat rocked. Eric laughed and hung on tight.

It would be a perfect celebration, Ariel thought. It'll be the best of land and sea!